There's a Bear IN YOUR BOOK

Written by **TOM FLETCHER**

PUFFIN

For Buzz, Buddy and Max – T.F.

PUFFIN BOOKS

UK | USA | Canada | Ireland | Australia | India | New Zealand | South Africa

Puffin Books is part of the Penguin Random House group of companies whose
addresses can be found at global.penguinrandomhouse.com.

www.penguin.co.uk
www.puffin.co.uk
www.ladybird.co.uk

 Penguin
Random House
UK

First published 2022

001

Copyright © Tom Fletcher, 2022
Illustrated by Dynamo
Based on illustrations by Greg Abbott

The moral right of the author has been asserted

Printed in Italy

The authorized representative in the EEA is
Penguin Random House Ireland, Morrison Chambers,
32 Nassau Street, Dublin D02 YH68

A CIP catalogue record for this book is available from the British Library

ISBN: 978–0–241–46663–6

All correspondence to:
Puffin Books, Penguin Random House Children's
One Embassy Gardens, 8 Viaduct Gardens, London SW11 7BW

GOODNESS ME!

It looks as though somebody has had a big picnic
in your book – who could it be?

It's a bear.

A very full-up bear.

A very full-up and very tired bear.

This is a bear that needs a good sleep.

Shall we help Bear get ready for bed?

First, Bear needs a bath.
And for a bath you need lots of . . .

Wow!
That's a lot of bubble bath, Bear.

Let's give the book a good **Shake**
to make it super-duper bubbly,
then turn the page.

What a lot of bubbles!
There must be a very clean bear under there.

POP the bubbles . . .

then turn the page.

Well done! Bear is nice and clean.
But your book is very wet – and so is Bear.

What's the best way to dry a soggy bear?
I KNOW!

FLAP your book like a fan
and then turn the page.

WHOOSH!

Well, that's certainly got Bear dry!

Now turn the page to get Bear settled
down and snuggled into bed.

SHHH.

Look, Bear's all snuggled up.

GENTLY ROCK the book

SIDE TO SIDE

to lull Bear to sleep.

Well done – Bear is getting more and more sleepy.

I'm sure Bear will be asleep
by the time you turn the page . . .

BOO!

OH NO! A cheeky little monster
has woken Bear up. Naughty!

Show Monster how cross you are.
Wag your finger at him
and turn the page.

Aw – Monster looks sorry.

How about we let him stay in your book –
as long as he helps Bear get to sleep?

Let's make everything comfortable for them.

Can you **IMAGINE** some soft pillows
and a nice big night light?

Are you imagining? Good – now turn the page.

Great imagining!

Now let's make your book
even more cosy.

PRESS the switch to turn on Bear's night light, then turn the page.

That's better!
Your book feels much more cosy now.

And look –
Monster and Bear are settling down for bed.

Now do a big **YAWN!**

I bet that will make
Monster and Bear yawn too . . .

Great! Monster and Bear are yawning,
but they're not quite asleep.

YAAAWN!

Hmm – A really good way to get to sleep
is to count sheep.

Can you IMAGINE five sheep
for them to count?

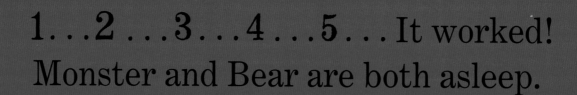

1...2...3...4...5... It worked!
Monster and Bear are both asleep.

But now there are all these
SHEEP in your book!

Can you help them fall asleep too?

Let's sing them a lullaby . . .

Twinkle, twinkle, little sheep,
time for you to go to sleep!

SHHHHHH!
Great work – now everyone's asleep.

Or nearly everyone . . .

Close the book quickly
before SOMEONE makes a noise!

Sleep tight!